STRIVE TO SURVIVE
YOU DECIDE WHAT HAPPENS

Deadly Expedition

Written by
Jeanne Gowen Dennis and Sheila Seifert

Cover illustration by David Hohn
Interior illustrations by Ron Adair

W9-BRY-052

www.cookcommunications.com/kidz

Faith Building Guide

Ages 9 and up

Faith

Faith Kidz® is an imprint of Cook Communications Ministries
Colorado Springs, Colorado 80918
Cook Communications, Paris, Ontario
Kingsway Communications, Eastbourne, England

DEADLY EXPEDITION!
©2003 by Jeanne Gowen Dennis and Sheila Seifert

First printing, 2003
Printed in U.S.A.
1 2 3 4 5 6 7 8 9 10 Printing/Year 07 06 05 04 03

Senior Editor: Heather Gemmen
Design Manager: Jeffrey P. Barnes
Designer: Granite Design

Have you ever wanted to witness the Red Sea opening or the walls of Jericho falling? The Strive to Survive series takes you into the middle of the action of your favorite Bible stories.

In each story, you are the main character. What happens is up to you! Through your choices, you can receive great rewards, get into big trouble, or even lose your life.

Your goal is to choose well and survive.
Your adventure begins now.

Deadly Expedition

"The Egyptians are coming! Help us! Moses, help us!" Everyone around you is screaming. You stand up on a cart to see over the heads of thousands of people around you—about 600,000 men and lots more women and children. In the distance you see a cloud of dust. Could it be Pharaoh's army? Only a couple of days ago, Pharaoh let you and all the other Israelite slaves go free. Why would he have changed his mind?

Your younger sisters, Mary and Mariah, are screaming. They are identical twins with identical high-pitched shrills. They sound a lot younger than their ten years.

"That's enough," your father says.

They cover their mouths with their hands, but their eyes remain large. You know that their hearts are probably beating as rapidly as yours. You strain your eyes to see in the distance as your mother tries to quiet your baby brother, Kilion. He is screaming, not from fear, but because he loves to yell.

You look back at the cloud of dust on the

distant horizon, then in the opposite direction at the Red Sea. Your hands feel clammy. There is nowhere to go! Your escape route is blocked by water!

"Now what?" you ask.

"Moses must have a plan," your mother says. "He wouldn't bring us here to die." You hear uncertainty in her voice. She hands you a crust of bread, the last of the bread that she baked at your home in Egypt. It is stale, almost without taste, but you gnaw on it as the others in your family struggle to eat their pieces of bread.

A man shouts to Moses, "Why did you bring us all the way into the desert to die? Didn't Egypt have enough graves?"

A woman adds, "It would have been better to remain slaves in Egypt than to die out here."

Mary and Mariah begin to scream again in their high-pitched voices, "We're going to die! We're going to die!"

CHOICE ONE: If you agree with your sisters and begin yelling, turn to page 94.

CHOICE TWO: If you tell your sisters to be quiet so you can hear what Moses is saying, turn to page 7.

Your father leans forward toward a friend. "Can you tell what Moses is saying?"

"I sent Esau to the front," the friend says. "He'll tell us."

You watch Moses until he has finished talking. Then you spot Esau in the crowd, weaving his way back to his family at a run. He has been your best friend since you were little.

When he gets close, his father yells, "Well? What did he say? How are we supposed to escape?"

Esau holds up a hand and tries to catch his breath. The cloud of dust behind you from the approaching chariots is enormous, darkening the entire horizon.

"He told us to stand firm and watch to see how God delivers us," Esau answers. "He said that the Lord would fight for us, and we need only to be still."

Your mother shakes her head. "Then that's that." She does not stop Kilion from yelling. Your father looks away. Mary and Mariah scream.

Esau's father scoffs. "I've seen how God provides." He points to the welts on his back. "I've seen it my whole life."

You have welts, too, from being beaten. Your muscles still ache from bending over to make Egyptian bricks these last several years. Why did you believe Moses? When he talked about taking everyone to the Promised Land, you had such high hopes. You dreamed of being free and having plenty to eat.

You wonder how you ever thought you could get to the "land flowing with milk and honey."

"Is all hope lost?" you ask to no one in particular as you step down from the cart.

Your father puts his arm around your shoulders, "I don't know. God did send plagues of frogs, locusts, and blood-filled water to our enemies."

Your mother adds, "And he punished the Egyptians by killing their first-born sons." They look at each other as if trying to believe. You turn away from your family and look at the pillar-like cloud that shows God is with you. The screams around you are increasing. Pharaoh's army is drawing nearer.

CHOICE ONE: If you wait to see how God provides, go to page 9.

CHOICE TWO: If you take matters in your own hands, go to page 12.

"I think we should listen to Moses," you tell your mother and give her what you hope is an encouraging smile. "It's going to be okay." Your mother nods, but then bites her top lip and looks down.

"Rhoda, we'll be fine," your father repeats. Your parents' eyes meet. You turn away from them and hear a sound as if a strong wind is blowing. Your eyes settle on the pillar of cloud again. Is it moving?

"Look!" you say, pointing to it. "The pillar of cloud!" That cloud has led you every day and then turned into a pillar of fire at night to guide you. Moses says that the pillar is God leading his people, and that you are one of his people. Every time the cloud has moved, you have moved. Every time it has stopped, you have camped and eaten gritty food— food coated with desert sand. Again, you are amazed at the cloud's enormous size. It looks like a desert windstorm piled up in a column.

"The cloud!" another voice yells. Soon everyone is watching God's pillar. Slowly it moves around the entire Israelite camp. You can smell the muddy water near the shore of the Red Sea. When the cloud reaches the desert sand behind you, it spreads out like a wall.

"The Egyptians will never be able to get through that," Esau says. You agree. With the pillar of cloud between you and the Egyptians, you cannot even see the dust cloud that the Egyptians were making. You are glad. If you cannot see them, then they cannot see you.

A cheer goes up from the crowd.

Esau laughs. "That was cool."

Esau's father sneers. "Moses will probably say that the cloud is God protecting us. He tries to use everything to his advantage."

"You don't think God is protecting us?" you ask. Esau's father rolls his eyes.

Esau says, "Let's not worry about who did what. The cloud is between us and the Egyptians. That will give us some time to figure out what to do next."

The night grows dark behind the cloud, but on your side, the pillar of fire lights the whole camp. You do not like sitting still.

CHOICE ONE: If you continue waiting to see what God will do, go to page 77.

CHOICE TWO: If you begin figuring out what your family needs to do next, go to page 43.

Why would Moses lead all of these people into a trap? With the cold Red Sea on one side and Pharaoh's ferocious army bearing down on you from the other, there is nowhere to go.

"Moses must have been crazy to lead us here," you mutter to Esau. "He's not a skilled leader like the Egyptians were. We shouldn't have trusted him."

Esau nods. "Yeah, my dad is pretty upset about it, but what can we do?"

"I don't know, but I'll think of something."

Your parents are busy taking care of the younger kids. You cannot bear to see the worry in their faces. You are the eldest. You must figure out how to keep your family together and alive. The dust cloud in the distance is getting larger, which means that Pharaoh's army is getting closer. You can smell the dust in the air.

You slowly move away from your tent so that your family will not notice that you are leaving. You can think of only two possible ways to fix the situation.

CHOICE ONE: If you try to find an escape route for your family, go to page 13.

CHOICE TWO: If you throw yourself on the mercy of Pharaoh, go to page 92.

You spit into the sand at your feet. The time to trust others—Moses, Pharaoh, God—is gone. You take off running along the edge of the Red Sea. You are going to find a shallow place where you and your family can cross, even if it takes you all night.

After running for some time, you shout to the sea, "Tell me your secrets!" The water remains calm except for an occasional plop from an insect or rodent.

The sky darkens, but the pillar of fire in the distance gives you just enough light to see. You continue along the shoreline of the Red Sea. No matter how far you go, it is much too wide and deep for your family to cross safely because no one in your family knows how to swim. Besides, the wind has picked up, and waves have started forming.

You stop and try to catch your breath. Your mouth is dry, but the seawater smells like dead fish. You look into the darkness ahead of you and then back to the distant pillar of fire behind you.

CHOICE ONE: If you turn back and start looking for a place to cross in the opposite direction, go to page 48.

CHOICE TWO: If you keep going in the same direction until you find an escape route, go to page 36.

"Help!" you scream. You stand up, trip on a stone, and fall, hitting your chin on a jagged rock. Ignoring the pain, you scramble to get up. The sand slides beneath you, and you taste its dirty flavor once again. "Help!"

It is too late. The man is right behind you. You cannot escape him now. You shut your eyes to prepare for death, but suddenly, the man groans. Thump. It sounds like someone fell to the ground. Cautiously, you look behind you. An Israelite is standing over the enemy's body. He has saved you!

"Thank you!" you say. You want to cry, you are so happy.

"Run home," the Israelite says sternly. "This is no place for children."

You nod. There is nothing you want more than to run home. You slip around the body, and try to run away, but you are too sore. You limp toward camp. The scrape on your chin throbs with pain. Yet, all the way home, you take deep breaths of warm air and relish the smells of the desert plants. You feel grateful to be alive. You had no idea that battles were so dangerous.

When your father comes home that night, you volunteer to clean his sword. It is really heavy. You look the other way as you wipe the blood from it. The smell reminds you of the dead enemy soldier. You wrinkle your nose.

Afterwards you hold the sword just as the Israelite soldier did who saved your life. You try to use it, but it is too heavy. You want to be able to defend yourself if another enemy attacks. You pick it up again.

"No. No," says your father, laughing. "Hold it this way." He shows you. You mimic his hold. "That's better," he says. He shows you how to use it. From now on, you plan to practice every day. You do not know what lies ahead, but you want to be prepared.

THE END

You hate the sun. You hate the sand. You are tired of noise, and sick to death of eating manna at every meal. You see no reason why you should obey your parents and not be with your friends, but you decide to obey anyway.

After a few days of obeying, you find it easier to be grateful for what you have. Soon you choose not to complain, no matter how you feel. When your friends bug you, you try to remember what it felt like when you were on the other side of the Red Sea, away from them and God's pillar of protection. When you have to carry water and it sloshes onto your clothes, or you collect manna when it is not supposed to be your turn, you try to remember how much harder it was making bricks as a slave. Besides, water sliding down your throat is a great feeling in a desert; and manna has a honey-sweet smell that is almost like perfume.

"Why are you such a goody-two-sandals?" Esau asks you one day.

You shrug and shake your head. "I get as discouraged as you do, but I also know that without God, life is a lot worse."

Esau looks at you strangely, but he starts hanging around you more than he used to. As long as he does not complain, you let him.

You can ignore the complaints outside your tent, but it is harder to ignore the ones inside. Almost every day, Mary says, "Do we have to eat manna again?"

"It's a wonderful gift from God," you say. "You know, when I was—"

"Oh please," says Mariah holding up her hands. "Not that story about almost starving to death. I don't have to be grateful about eating the same thing every day just because you were hungry once."

Mary makes a disgusted sound. "Come along, Mariah. Let's go find Leah."

The next morning, you are determined to keep quiet as you gather manna with your sisters. You look up at the sky.

You say, "Isn't it great how God sends us manna to eat every morning?"

Mariah yells, "Mother! I'm getting another lecture on being grateful for what I have." As the twins hurry away from you, you shake your head. Your mother comes up behind you and rubs your back.

"Everyone's complaining nowadays," she says.

"But we have it so easy," you say. "God has really blessed us. We're free, we have food and water, and God loves us."

Then one day, your father comes to you. "Let's talk about everything God has done for us. I'm tired and discouraged. I just need to hear it one more time."

From then on, you do not care what people say. You tell everyone who will listen about how wonderful God is.

THE END

"I would like to travel with you for a while," you say. "And I want to work to pay for my food and my place in this caravan; but if we ever travel to the other side of the sea, I must try to find my family."

"Of course," Haran says.

"And perhaps you could even help me find out where my people might have gone." You give Haran a hopeful smile.

Haran throws back his head and laughs. "And what brings more pleasure in life than going out of one's way for a stranger? We will help you find your people, Little Pilgrim."

"Thank you," you say. You travel with them for many days across the hot desert and realize that Haran is going quite a bit out of his way to help you. He sends out scouts to try to find news of Israel's people. You are amazed at the man's generosity. In some ways, you almost hope that you will not have to leave Haran's caravan.

You have grown used to eating horsemeat and drinking tea. Many camels are laden with sacks full of goods. The sacks still smell like the spices that Haran traded for the goods. Even the barking of the caravan's dogs, and the strange words of the traders are beginning to sound familiar, although you do not yet understand their language. In spite of all of this, there is an ache in your heart that will continue until you find your family.

Then one day, Haran calls you to him, "Little Pilgrim," he says, "We have found your people. He

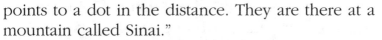

points to a dot in the distance. They are there at a mountain called Sinai."

"You are certain it is the Israelites?" you ask.

Haran nods and then looks at you closely. "Are you certain that you wish to leave us?"

You shake your head. "I do not wish to leave you, but my place is with my people."

"A good answer," Haran says. "May the gods be with you, Little Pilgrim."

"May the God of Moses bless you for your kindness to me," you answer. Haran nods his head once to receive your blessing. Then he gives you food and water for a day's journey.

As you leave the caravan, a lump catches in your throat. Just then Haran yells, "If you change your mind, Little Pilgrim, you can find us to the east."

"And if you wish to join my people," you call back, "you will always be welcome at my family's table."

Your heart is lighter as you continue on your way. You reach the camp in the late afternoon, but are surprised at what you see. A smoky cloud hangs over the mountain, and dead bodies are everywhere. It looks as if at least 3,000 men have been killed in some kind of battle. You think that an enemy must have come down and attacked your people. You are wrong. These people all turned against God and worshipped an idol.

As you help bury the dead, you keep looking for signs of your family. No one seems to know where they are. You hope they are all right. You search for your family's tent.

Finally, you see one in the distance with colorful decorations all over it. Only Mary and Mariah would decorate a tent like that. You run toward it. As you draw closer, you hear voices.

"If you save any manna over night, it will turn into bugs," Mariah says.

"That's not true," Mary says. "That only happened to Naomi. What if I get hungry in the night?"

"Girls," your mother says in a stern tone. "Get rid of those pieces of honey-bread now. I will not have maggots living in our tent with us."

Mary exits the tent first and sees you. She gives a high-pitched squeal, which is soon joined by Mariah's screams. "You're back! You're back!"

You give them each a hug as your mother comes out of the tent to see what the commotion is. You hear a sob catch in her throat and then her arms wrap around you. Behind her, your father waits to greet you.

"We thought the Egyptians had killed you," your father says. He gives you a bear hug around your mother when she refuses to let you go. You wipe tears from your eyes. When you are finally able to stand back and look at your family, you see that they have all grown thinner, and there are dark circles around your parents' eyes.

As Moses leaves to go up Mount Sinai again, you and your family spend a lot of time with each other. You tell your family about your experiences, and they tell you about everything you missed. The people made a covenant, a serious agreement, with God. Those who died had broken the covenant.

The God of Moses scares you. This God is even more powerful than you imagined, and deadly. Being with Haran was so much easier.

CHOICE ONE: If you stay with Israel, go to page 80.

CHOICE TWO: If you leave to find Haran, go to page 41.

You decide to go with your friends. As you wave goodbye to Caleb, you ask your friends, "Is snake hunting safe?"

"Sure," your friend says. "Eight of us are going. We'll bring home lots of meat so we don't have to eat manna all the time."

You hunt for days. Although you see a lot of snakes, none of you are quick enough to catch them. After days of unsuccessful snake hunting, you are all starving. On the last day, you almost get a snake with your knife before it rears up and hisses at you. You jump back. It strikes, but it only gets the air. As you run from it, you think, "That's it for me. Manna is better than this!" Your friends run back toward camp with you. The whole way, all you can think about is eating those sweet-tasting wafers.

By the time you reach the camp, Moses has returned, and it looks like all of Israel is getting ready to leave. Tents are being taken down; dogs are barking; sheep are bleating. A camel spits at you as you walk by it. You are glad to be home.

"You got back just in time," your father says. "How did the hunting go?"

"Don't ask," you say. Your father laughs.

Mary says, "You missed all the excitement."

"You should've seen what Moses looked like when he came down from the mountain," Mariah says. But the twins refuse to say anything else.

You help break camp for the big journey ahead to the Promised Land.

THE END

You are so tired that you fall down by your family's things. Sand gets into your mouth. It is still warm from the day, but you are too tired to even spit it out. You know the situation is hopeless. You shut your eyes.

Mariah says, "Mary, if I die, you may have my favorite blue bead."

"You just can't die," Mary wails. "If the Egyptians separate us, I'll always remember you. You are my best twin in the whole world."

"She's your only twin," you mutter into the sand just before you fall asleep. Someone pulls on your arm.

"Stop it!" you say. It's probably Mariah and Mary bugging you again. You turn over. The desert sand feels gritty against your skin.

"Get up now," your mother's voice says. It sounds far away. Someone keeps pulling your arm.

"I don't want to wake up just to die," you mumble.

Someone pinches your ear. "Ow!" You open one eyelid. Your mother is holding Kilion with one hand and your ear with the other. You cannot figure out what is going on. Your legs are heavy.

"We have to walk," she says, but her voice is distant. You would nod your head, but her fingers hold your earlobe in place.

"Just let me sleep a little more," you beg, wondering why the dream seems so real.

"Stop your complaining," she says. Your mother

usually is not so demanding. This has to be a dream.

You follow her, or at least follow in the direction your ear is being pulled, because you do not have a choice. For being in the middle of a dream, your earlobe sure hurts, and your legs ache. You stub your toe on a rock and get dirt in your sandals. This dream journey seems to take forever. You are in some strange kind of tunnel or something like a tunnel, but the sky is still above you. Is that a fish you just saw swimming above your head on the left? Maybe you are drowning.

"I don't know how to swim!" you yell. You feel a harder pinch on your earlobe. Then you feel hands tugging on your arms. Are the twins both trying to wake you up now? You seem to be going up a hill. Finally, the pressure on your ear is gone. You fall into a dreamless sleep.

A loud roaring sound wakes you up. All the people are crowded around you looking in the same direction. You stand up and see two huge waves crashing together on the sea, and are those chariot wheels? Suddenly, you realize that you are on the other side of the Red Sea from where you fell asleep.

"How did I get here?" you ask. The twins are giggling.

"You swam across," Mary teases.

"No, you really rode across on a crocodile's back," Mariah adds. "I was so frightened for you."

"Good one, Mariah," Mary says, patting her on the back.

"I liked yours, too," Mariah said.

"No more of these late nights for you," says your mother. "God opened the sea, and we all walked across."

You walked across the Red Sea. So the fish above you was not a dream. You wish you could remember it more clearly. Everyone is talking about the miracle God did for Israel. You can see dead Egyptian soldiers floating in the water. You realize that God just defeated the powerful and scary Egyptian army in a few moments. Seeing the force of that water, you are glad that you did not have to swim across.

Moses' sister, Miriam, starts singing a song of praise to the Lord. Children and women dance along the edge of the sea, rejoicing that they are safe. You are so excited that you start praising this God Moses has told everyone about, the one who calls himself I AM. You choose to follow him.

THE END

You look at the huge basket and feel embarrassed. You return it to the tent and get one that holds an omer. You hand Kilion a piece of manna. He stuffs it into his mouth. He does not have teeth yet, but he gums at the manna, smiling. "Mmmm." His saliva drips down his face.

As you fill your basket, you taste the manna over and over. You try to figure out what it is made out of, but the flavor is like nothing you have eaten before. It smells sweet and tastes a little like your mother's honey bread, only much better. It feels light and flaky.

From that day on, the manna comes every morning. You pick up only the amount that you will eat for that day, except on the day before the Sabbath. Then you collect enough for two days. Some people eat manna as it is, and others find all kinds of ways to fix it—manna cakes, manna crackers, manna burgers. It truly is an amazing food.

It is now three months since you left Egypt. You set up a camp near the base of Mount Sinai. It feels good to rest from traveling. Shortly after you arrive, you watch Moses start up the mountain to meet with God.

"Yeah, right," Esau says. "Like God lives on top of a mountain."

You laugh. "I think Moses said that God was going to meet him up there at the top."

"Well, good riddance," Esau says. "I'm tired of Moses telling us what to do all the time."

Mary and Mariah count the days that Moses has been gone. Life in camp becomes a dull routine.

"Moses has been gone thirty-three days," Mariah says one morning.

"No, I'm positive that he left thirty-eight days ago," says Mary.

You shrug. Moses has been gone a long, long time.

"He's probably dead," your father says slowly. You hope Moses is safe. If he is not, then what will happen to all of you? You look up at the cloud that hovers at the top of Mount Sinai.

Esau's father and some other men collect gold jewelry from the people. They want to make a god to worship like the ones the Egyptians had. They even ask your mother for her jewelry to melt down for their idol!

"Please don't give it to them," cries Mary. Mariah is sobbing so hard that she cannot speak. Mary continues, "Don't you love us? If you give that to them, what will we have for a dowry?"

Your mother rolls her eyes, but she refuses to give her jewelry. The jewelry was from your Egyptian masters. They gave it to her just before you left Egypt. Esau's father and some of the other men talk Aaron into making a calf out of the gold they collected.

Once it is made, Esau runs over to you. "You're missing out on a good time!"

You shrug. "What's going on?'

"I'm going to go and give homage to the golden calf," Esau says. He looks excited.

"You're going to what?" you ask.

"It looks just like the god that Ramsey had outside of his palace. Do you remember the one that we could just see from the top of the hill?" Esau says. "Now that's a god for you. That's the kind of god we should worship."

"You don't really believe that, do you?" you ask.

"Don't you?" Esau asks. "Come on. Moses is dead. It's time for us to get on with our lives. Are you coming?"

CHOICE ONE: If you refuse to worship the golden calf, go to page 67.

CHOICE TWO: If you go with Esau, go to page 50.

Thinking does not help. You do not understand, but you know that what Esau and his father did was wrong. You find your father. He holds out his arms to you, and you rush into them, sobbing.

"I don't like it when people die," you say.

"I don't either," your father says.

"Why did Esau have to die?" you cry. Your father holds you in his arms, and you draw comfort from him.

After a while, your father says, "I don't know why Esau chose to rebel against God. I don't know why his father taught him to rebel. What I do know is that God is God."

Your heart is heavy, but seeing how Esau ended up helps you make a decision. You will spend your life doing whatever God wants you to do. Even though you still grumble and complain sometimes on your long trip through the desert, you ask God for forgiveness when you do.

When you are 52 years old, you watch the swollen waters of the Jordan River part, and you remember how God made a path for you through the Red Sea when you were only a child. Your life-long dream comes true. You cross the Jordan River into the Promised Land, the "land flowing with milk and honey." Mary, Mariah, and Kilion are glad to get there, too. But even at age 50, Mary is afraid of the bees that make the honey.

THE END

"Please, may I ride with you?" you beg. You really do not want to be trampled by the other chariots.

"You'll slow me down," says your master.

"I'm light," you say. "Your horse will never know I'm here. Besides, a man who is as good a charioteer as you are won't even notice a little more weight. From what I saw yesterday, you must be the best charioteer in Pharaoh's army."

Your master smiles. "Well said, young one. Hop on for the ride of your life!"

You understand what he means when the chariot begins moving forward. The air rushes past you. The chariot feels like it is flying as it bumps over the sand. Your heart races. In your chest, you feel a kind of excitement that you have never felt before. You can hardly breathe. You grip the edge of the chariot.

In only moments, you have reached the Red Sea. You bump down into the seabed. The walls of water on either side tower over you. Even in your master's grand chariot, you feel small and unimportant.

"I've seen many things," your master yells back at you, "but never this. This God of Israel is great, but the gods of Egypt are greater."

"I'm not so sure about that," you say. You remember the plagues in Egypt. In the distance, you watch Moses pointing his staff at the sea from a cliff.

"Uh-oh," you say. The walls of water collapse.

The force of the water slams your head against the side of the chariot and buries you in the sea.

THE END

You decide that rocks are no match for swords. You stay hidden. From where you are perched, you can see that Moses has his hands up. Now and then, he lowers his arms—probably to let some blood flow back into them. Every time he does, Israel starts losing. When he lifts them up again, Israel pushes ahead.

After a while, you can tell that Moses is getting tired, because his arms are falling down more often. You panic. Someone needs to do something! Then Aaron, Moses' brother, and Hur, a leader of Israel, stand on either side of Moses and hold up his arms until sunset.

Israel wins, and you raise your arms like Moses and praise God. You feel sure that he will get you safely to the Promised Land. You cannot wait to taste the milk, honey, and all the wonderful foods there. Mariah says that rich food will be bad for her complexion. Mary is afraid of the bees that will make the honey. You are not. God has been good to Israel. He chose the Promised Land for you. You choose to believe that it will be a wonderful place. You cannot wait to get there.

THE END

"Pharaoh's army is coming too fast!" you say to yourself. You are afraid that they will not notice that you are there. You change your mind and begin running back toward the Israelite camp. As you run, your eyes latch onto the pillar of cloud that God has used to guide Israel to the Red Sea. Suddenly, it is moving toward you. It stops directly between you and the Israelite camp. You can no longer smell the campfires.

"Oh no!" you yell. Your way back to camp is cut off. The Egyptian army is close behind you. You close your eyes and wait to be trampled to death.

Instead of being trampled, you hear chariot wheels grinding to a halt, horses whinnying in fear, and men shouting.

"Is it a sandstorm?" a loud voice asks.

"Can we get through it?" another yells. You open your eyes. No one seems to notice you. One Israelite child alone could not be much of a threat. You take a step away from them.

An important looking officer says, "First line, forward." An entire section of chariots tries to move forward, but the horses will not get any nearer to the cloud. They back up no matter how hard their masters whip them.

One man jumps down from his chariot and charges right into the cloud with a battle cry. Everyone waits. And waits. And waits. The man never returns.

CHOICE ONE: If you run up to a soldier in one of the chariots and beg for mercy, go to page **86**.

CHOICE TWO: If you try to run around the cloud, go to page **66**.

You run all the next day. You are afraid that the Egyptians have already reached your family. If that is true, then you are all alone. You are the only Israelite who has survived the Egyptians. If your family is not dead, they are certainly slaves again. The thought brings you such sorrow that you begin to cry. Your eyes become blurred. You cannot tell where you are going anymore, so you stop, fall to your knees, and cover your face with your rough hands.

When you can cry no longer, you remove your hands and wipe your nose with your sleeve. In the distance you see a caravan. You feel an ache inside. You do not want to live the rest of your life alone. You run toward the caravan, hoping they are not a mirage. The gnawing pain in your stomach reminds you that you have not eaten solid food since you left your father's tent.

"Please, kind Travelers," you yell once you are within range, "I wish to go with you, wherever you are going."

A man with twinkling eyes and a ready smile says, "We are traders headed for the Far East."

"Are you really?" you ask. When you were a slave, you would see exotic travelers passing by but never dreamed that you would be able to travel with them and see the rest of the world. You have always wondered what lies beyond Egypt.

"You look like a sturdy traveler." The caravan leader smiles.

You stand up taller. "I am. I would like to join your caravan. I will work, of course."

"Good. We are in need of workers."

Over the years as you journey with these merchants, you see many amazing sights. Every once in a while, you hear rumors about how God saved his people, the Israelites, from the Egyptians. You wonder if the rumors are true and if you should have stayed with them. You will never know.

THE END

Where will you find food? Where will you find water? For three days, you wander with the rest of Israel. Blisters swell on your feet and make you limp. Your meals are getting smaller and smaller. Your growling stomach makes you grumpy, and the twins are annoying you with their complaining.

"I'm hungry. My stomach huuuurts!" Mary says, stretching out the last word for effect. Mariah is upset because the shine has left her hair.

At a place called Marah you find water, but your hopes are dashed. It is too bitter to drink.

"It's all Moses' fault," Esau's father complains. Everyone grumbles.

You join them. "Moses, why did you lead us out into the desert to die of thirst?"

You watch Moses ask God about it. Then Moses throws a stick into the water. It turns the water sweet. You guzzle the cool water, letting some spill on your face and drip down your neck. You feel a little hopeful. Moses solved the water problem, for now; but when will he solve the food problem?

"This isn't how I pictured the journey to the Promised Land," Esau says.

"We'll die of starvation or foot sores before we get there," you say.

Your parents seem to be taking things pretty well.

"One thing at a time," your father says. Your mother nods her head in agreement and tries to comfort you, your brother, and your sisters. But every now and then you see worry lines in her face.

One day Esau's father says, "We ate our last food this morning. Moses brought us into the wilderness to die."

The whole camp is saying the same thing. "Why didn't we just die in Egypt?"

Then Moses tells everyone, "God will send food from the sky."

Can you believe him?

"This evening you will have meat," Moses continues. "In the morning God will rain bread from the sky. Take only as much as you can eat for the day. On the day before the Sabbath, gather enough for two days."

That evening, thousands of quail cover the camp. You stuff yourself and go to bed full for the first time since you can remember. You dream of cows, birds, leeks, and melons falling from the sky. One cow falls onto your tent, right on top of you. You wake up. It was not a cow. The twins are jumping on you.

"What are you doing?" you demand.

"You've got to come and see what God sent for breakfast," Mariah says. "I don't know if it'll be good for my figure or not, but it really tastes good."

"It's sweet like honey," Mary says. "And there are no bees."

Your sisters hurry out of the tent. You sit up and squint at the bright light coming through the flaps. Covering the ground are thin flakes of something white. People everywhere are gathering them. You get dressed and go outside.

Your sisters are collecting the white flakes. This mysterious food goes into their mouths as well as their baskets. You pick up a flake and taste it. Your eyes open wide. It is delicious. It is like a sweet cracker or bread. You have never tasted anything like it.

Mary calls, "Mother, Mariah and I each have an omer. Can we go play now?"

"Go ahead," your mother says. She turns to you. "Collect only as much manna as you can eat today. I'll get enough for Kilion, your father, and me."

"Okay," you say. You grab a great big basket. You have a really large appetite.

Moses calls out to remind people, "Take only what you need. Do not save any until morning."

CHOICE ONE: If you do what Moses says, go to page 26.

CHOICE TWO: If you ignore Moses and take all you want, go to page 89.

The God of Moses frightens you. The burning mountain that others call Sinai is scary. What if the fire should leave the top and attack the ground where your tents are? Although you are glad to be with other Israelites, they are not how you remembered them.

"This stinks," someone said the first day you were back.

"What stinks?" you asked. You sniffed the air thinking he meant the smoke from the mountain.

"Living like this," he said.

Now several days later, you look around you. Everyone has a place to stay. God provides manna for people to eat every morning. No foreign army is attacking. What are these people complaining about? They seem to have everything! Do they want to go back to Egypt? You do not! Have they forgotten what it was like being slaves? You are tired of listening to all their complaints.

Mary groans, "How much longer must we live like this?"

"That's enough!" you say. You almost wish Haran had never found the Israelite camp. Your heart longs for his merry ways.

"What's your problem?" Mariah asks.

"You and the others complain all the time," you say. "Yet you have everything you need. Traveling with Haran's caravan was tough, but his people stayed pleasant."

"Touchy. Touchy," says Mariah.

"And if there was a dangerous mountain with fire on it, Haran wouldn't be camping by it," you say.

"Are you scared?" asks Mary. She begins to taunt, "Scaredy-cat! Scaredy-cat!"

The rest of the day, you compare Haran's camp to Israel's camp. Later that night, you tell your father, "I want to go east and find Haran."

He shakes his head. "You would leave the God of Israel?"

"I want to leave the grumbling and complaining," you say. "I don't know what is going on here with fire on the mountain, but I want to leave."

When you leave your family, everyone cries, including you, but leaving the other Israelites is not hard at all. You head east. You never find Haran's caravan. The next caravan owner you meet is not so nice. You become his slave for life.

THE END

The Egyptians are waiting for you on the other side of the pillar of cloud. No one knows when or where the pillar will move, and danger lurks behind it.

"What am I doing sitting here?" you think. "I've got to get across that sea before tomorrow."

You ask your parents, "Can you teach me how to swim?"

"I don't know how," your mother says as she holds your sleeping brother to her chest.

Your father shakes his head. "When would we have had the chance to learn? The Egyptians kept us working so hard, we didn't have time. Besides, swimming in crocodile-infested waters didn't really appeal to me."

You laugh nervously. You go and ask another family camped near yours, "Do you know how to swim?" They do not know either. You go to the next family and then the next.

Most of the adults are packing up to leave. They do not have time to spend talking to you.

"Why do you want to swim?" one man asks, not really expecting an answer.

You turn away. The pillar is lighting up the whole camp, and it hardly seems like night. Finally, you give up trying to find a swimming teacher and stumble toward where your family is camped.

CHOICE ONE: If you stay awake the rest of the night, go to page 70.

CHOICE TWO: If you go to sleep, go to page 23.

"Go have fun," you say. "I'll just hang out here."
Esau leaves, and you stay where you are and watch.
The crowd in front of the calf looks too rowdy to be
safe. Besides, you do not want your parents getting
more upset with you. You have not been getting
along very well lately. You watch for quite a while.
The people look like little children dancing around
the calf.

Suddenly, you see Moses coming down the
mountain. He smashes some stone tablets on the
rocks and looks really angry. He grabs the golden
calf and grinds it to powder. Then he spreads it on
the water. He makes everyone drink some, even you.
It makes you gag. As you are choking, you hear
Moses ask Aaron why he did it.

"It wasn't my fault!" Aaron says. "The people
didn't know what happened to you. You know how
easily they slip back into doing evil."

Moses did not look convinced.

"I only asked them to take off their gold jewelry.
Then I threw it into the fire, and out popped this
golden calf."

"Oh brother!" you think. You cannot believe that
Aaron is telling such a whopper of a lie. I guess
that's what happens when you listen to the wrong
people.

You are going to stay away from people who
disobey God from now on. It is not worth it. You
clear the last particles of that horrible gold from
your throat, and decide that you will never worship

any god except the real God.

THE END

The dust is flying up around Pharaoh's army. How will they be able to see you? Thinking quickly, you untie the white cloth from your head and wave it with all your might. Your waving arms make a cool breeze around you. You stand on your tiptoes to make yourself taller. Surely the white cloth will get the attention of Pharaoh's lead charioteers.

You glance back at the Israelite camp. They look so far away. You turn back to watch Pharaoh's chariots. They are bearing down on you. They are traveling so fast. They do not even slow down! You are able to dodge one by jumping to the side. You roll out of the path of another. Unfortunately, you roll directly into the path of the horse pulling the next chariot. You are trampled to death.

THE END

You are tired from running. You turn around and head back to the campsite. Your efforts have been in vain, and you are exhausted. How will you ever have the strength to continue looking for a crossing? Tears stream down your face. You want to help, but you have been able to do nothing.

At first light, you reach what should have been the camp, but no one is there. Just then, you see someone by the Red Sea. You hurry to the edge.

"Wait," you cry. "Where is everyone?"

You are amazed at what you see. It looks like there is a canyon of dry land right down the middle of the Red Sea. You can smell the fish. Some people are running along the bottom. How can this be happening? You see figures way in the distance on the opposite bank. It's hard to tell who they are, but you think that it must be the Israelites. The runners are getting close to the other shore. You have to catch up!

You take a deep breath. You cannot figure out what is keeping the water from splashing down on you. You hear a noise behind you. God's pillar of cloud is lifting. The Egyptian chariots are heading toward you. Your heart is beating wildly.

CHOICE ONE: If you go back and run along the seaside from which you came, go to page **84.**

CHOICE TWO: If you turn and run harder into the middle of the Red Sea, go to page **57.**

"It's just jewelry in the shape of a baby cow," you say. "Don't give me that god stuff."

"Come on," Esau says. "We're just trying to have some fun."

"I'm sure everyone is tired and bored like I am," you think. "I'm sure they all know the calf isn't really God." The more you think about what they are doing, the less you see wrong with it. They are not really hurting anything, not really. You see that your parents are not looking. You sneak away with Esau.

Some people are remaining in their tents. When you reach the area where the golden calf is standing, you see people everywhere. A lot of the women are wearing clothes that belonged to the Egyptians. They do not cover their bodies as well as they should. The men are just as bad. They have made something to drink, which is making them act very silly. You wonder how grown people can behave so foolishly.

"Come on," Esau says. He pushes his way through to the front of the pack and bows low before the golden calf. You look around you. You wish you were anywhere but here.

From his position on the ground, he says, "Don't embarrass me. Bow down. Everyone will think you're an ally of Moses if you don't worship our new god."

You give the golden image an awkward bow and then hurry away. The next day it is not as hard to bow down, and the following day, you bow all the way to the ground. Of course you and Esau

laugh about it later, as if acting silly in front of a golden calf is not a big deal.

Then one day, Moses returns. The glow on his face frightens you. He looks really angry. He destroys the golden calf, and many die by the sword for worshipping it and leading people the wrong way.

It is not until you are dying of a plague—a painful illness—a few days later, that you realize how horrible you were acting. You were unfaithful to the real God. Now you are paying for your terrible sin. You ask God for forgiveness before you die.

THE END

When you return to your family's tent, your father comes out to meet you.

"Moses killed my friend," you yell. "How could he? Why did God save us from Egypt to kill us here?"

Your father holds you close to him. "Moses didn't kill anyone. The sons of Levi fought against everyone who chose an idol instead of the living God. Esau and his father cursed God and said they would rather die."

"That's not what they meant," you say, pounding your hands against your father's chest. You cannot control your tears as they course down your cheeks. "I won't believe in a God who kills kids. I won't. I won't."

"God didn't want them to die," your father said. "They chose death over obedience to him."

You refuse to listen. From that day forward, you disobey the laws of God whenever you get the chance. You have an unhappy life. You die of a snakebite in the desert when you are thirty-five.

THE END

You decide that you need to do something to help Israel. You pick up a few rough stones and hurry closer to the battlefield. You see an enemy soldier below you. Sweat trickles down your back as you wait for him to get closer to where you are hiding. When he is close enough, you throw a stone, but it misses his head. He looks in your direction. You throw another stone. It hits his shoulder just as an Israelite soldier comes up behind him. Yes!

Suddenly, you hear someone behind you. You look over your shoulder. It is an Amalekite. You grab another stone and throw it as hard as you can. It hits him on the side of the head. He pauses, but the rock does not stop him. He darts toward you.

CHOICE ONE: If you shout for help, go to page 14.

CHOICE TWO: If you drop to the ground and roll toward the man's legs, go to page 69.

You know you will be in the way. You do not want to be trampled by the horses, so you hurriedly weave your way in and out of chariots until you are able to reach the back of the army where the servants are. You breathe a sigh of relief when you reach them.

"You are Baala's new slave?" asks a man who keeps his nose high in the air. You nod warily. "I am Baala's head servant," he says. "From now on, you will take orders from me. Call me 'Your Highness.' Do you understand, Slave?"

You nod but do not say anything. The man keeps talking and talking and talking about what you have to do. There must be more rules at Baala's house than in all the rest of Egypt! You nod every now and then while he talks, but keep your eyes on the charioteers. They are a mighty army, probably the strongest in the world. You almost feel a sense of pride at being Baala's slave. Serving a powerful person like him will have its benefits. When the Egyptians return with the Israelites, you will beg for your family's lives.

The servant keeps talking, but you no longer pay attention. Far in the distance, you see that the entire Egyptian army has entered the opening in the Red Sea. Suddenly, without warning, the sea closes in over the Egyptians with a crashing wave.

"Oh no!" you say as others around you begin shrieking. A few of the servants run toward the Red Sea. The slaves run in the opposite direction. You notice that the head servant with all of the rules is running away with the slaves.

At that moment, you cannot help but say, "Moses' God is God. He saved all of Israel."

You start running toward the Red Sea. The thick sand cannot keep you from your task. You want to find a way around the sea. You want to be with Israel and their God, a God as powerful as this deserves your loyalty.

It takes many days to find a way around the sea. For ten years, you wander in the desert looking for your family. You get really tired of eating locusts. Finally, one morning you wake behind a sand dune to find a white flaky substance all over the ground. You are examining it when someone comes over the dune with a basket.

"Mariah!" you shout. She drops her basket and runs to you.

You have never been so happy to see anyone before. You join your family in the Israelite camp and serve the God of Israel for the rest of your life.

THE END

You take a deep breath and sprint down the Red
Sea path toward the other side. You are tired, but
you have never run as fast as you are running now.
No matter what happens, you do not want to be left
behind. Your lungs burn as you race to catch up
with your family. Most of the other Israelites are
already on the other shore. You hear the thunder of
hooves and the rattle of chariots behind you.

You try to get more air into your lungs, but you
can hardly breathe. You push yourself forward with
long strides. Your feet pound the dry earth beneath
you. Just four more steps. Now three.

Suddenly the wind roars, and you sense the wall
of water falling. Two more steps. The shore is a blur
in front of you. You strain to reach it, but you feel
water splashing your legs. You are being swept
away!

"Help!" you call out, but know that it is too late.
Then you feel a strong hand grabbing your arm. The
next thing you know, your father has pulled you
from the water. You are safe! You hug your father,
laughing and crying at the same time. You do not
want to leave the safety of his arms.

After a praise celebration to thank God, you
continue your travels to the Promised Land. For
weeks, you and the other Israelites travel under the
scorching desert sun. You wish you had your house
in Egypt to protect you. God sends you manna,
bread from the sky, to eat every day, but you miss
the cool, juicy melons and cucumbers of past meals.

Lots of people are missing Egypt, just as you are. You are not used to traveling like this.

"Let's go find something else to eat," Esau says one morning. When your parents give you permission, you both go hunting with a group of others.

After you find nothing, the leader of the group says, "We could go back to camp if anyone knows where it is."

"What?" exclaims Esau. "Are we lost?" The leader nods his head. As you search for your families, you go an entire week without food.

"What's that in the distance?" you ask one day.

"It's our families!" cries your leader. Even in your weakened condition, you all run as fast as you can to the camp. From then on, manna tastes pretty good.

Soon, you camp in front of a mountain called Sinai. God talks to Moses. Then Moses consecrates the people. He sets you all apart as holy for God. You feel really clean, from the inside. The next day, you help wash your family's clothes so you will be clean on the outside and ready to meet with God. By the time you are through, your hands feel raw.

The third morning, thunder is crashing and lightning slits the sky. The mountain has a thick cloud over it, and you hear a loud trumpet blast.

"What's that?" you ask, trying to cover the fact that your teeth are chattering.

"I hope we don't have to stand and listen to more people talking," says Mary.

"Mariah and Mary, stop talking like that," says your father. "Have you no fear of God?"

They look ashamed. Moses leads everyone to the base of the mountain. All but Moses must stay away from the holy mountain or die.

Going up the mountain is not even a temptation for you. Smoke billows from Mount Sinai like smoke from a blazing furnace. The whole mountain is shaking as if it will erupt or split apart at any moment. Even though you are standing at a distance with the rest of the crowd, you want to turn and run. Moses actually starts up the mountain to talk with God! You are afraid to look. He will probably be burned alive.

Soon, Moses comes down. Somehow he survived the dangerous mountain. He tells everyone what God said. "Do not make for yourselves gods of silver or gold." He tells you lots of other things God said, including that he will make your enemies run in fear. Then God calls Aaron and seventy-two others to the mountain to worship at a distance.

Later, Moses tells the people about God's words and laws. Everyone agrees saying, "Everything the Lord has said we will do."

God calls Moses up the mountain again. Aaron and Hur are left in charge. As you watch Moses enter the dark cloud, you wonder if you will ever see him again.

"No human could live through the raging fire on the top of the mountain!" you think.

Moses is barely gone before people start complaining. Aaron looks like he wants to run away from it all, too. The complaining builds week after week as Moses fails to return.

Esau says, "Moses isn't coming back, and now we're stuck here in the desert. I wish we were back in Egypt."

Another friend says, "Do you remember the wonderful things we had there?"

Your mother shakes her head and pulls you aside. "I don't want you hanging around Esau and his group of friends."

CHOICE ONE: If you obey your mother, go to page 16.

CHOICE TWO: If you hang around with your friends anyway, go to page 82.

You turn around and go north. As you stand at the edge of the sea, you question what you saw. Did it really happen? Shattered chariots and the bodies of horses and men on the shore take away your doubts. You stare across the sea, but see no one. Tears sting your eyes.

You walk farther north. You are so thirsty and tired that eventually, you fall face down on the ground, expecting never to wake up. You feel the sand gradually covering you like a grave. When you regain consciousness, cold water is being poured on your face. You drink in as much as you can.

Only after you have had your fill do you say, "Who are you? What are you doing?"

"So the dead comes back to life," says a strange man with a fiery jewel on his turban. He helps you sit up. His colorful robes make you dizzy. He offers you another drink.

"There, that's better. Bring the child some food," he calls, clapping his hands. You eat some kind of brown mush in a bowl. You do not care what it is. You gulp it down as quickly as you can get it into your mouth. Only when you are done do you remember your manners and say, "Thank you." The man laughs at your poor attempt at politeness.

"I am Haran," says the man. "Little Pilgrim, what are you doing out here in the desert all by yourself?"

"I was with Moses and all my people," you say, "but the Egyptian army came after us."

"You mean the powerful army of Pharaoh?"

"Yes. Pharaoh let us go, but then he sent his army after us. God held back the sea and everyone crossed through and then the water fell on all the Egyptians and killed them."

Haran laughs. "If you do not want to tell me the truth, just say so."

"But I am telling you the truth," you say.

He looks surprised. "Then why are you here?" he asks.

You hang your head. "I was trying to find a way across the sea so my family could escape. I got back too late."

Haran looks at you with pity in his eyes. "I do not know if I believe your story, but many things happen that I do not understand." He fingers the jewel on his turban. "It is difficult to get along in this world without family. You may travel with us if you like."

CHOICE ONE: If you go with Haran, turn to page 76.

CHOICE TWO: If you ask him to help you to the other side of the sea so you can find your family, go to page 18.

The party does look like lots of fun. What difference will it make? You will be careful. You stand up.

"Lead the way," you say.

You join the others around the golden calf. You feel a little guilty at first, but then you really get into it. Someone gives you a drink that makes you feel light-headed and dizzy. You bow down and worship the idol. Then you join in all the fun, laughing and carrying on any way you like.

After a while, you see Moses storming toward you. He grabs the calf. You do not care. You and your friends keep partying. Moses makes you drink something that tastes awful, but you follow it with more good food and drink. You do not even notice what is going on around you until you hear a loud voice shouting.

"Whoever is for the Lord, come to me." It is Moses. You and your friends just stand there.

"Who is he to come back and spoil all our fun?" Esau says.

You all agree and go back to your party. Suddenly, you realize that men with swords are killing lots of the people. One kills Esau. Then he kills you.

THE END

"No, you go ahead," you say. "I'm going to stay around here."

"You can't tell me that you want to eat more manna," Esau exclaims

You shrug. "It's not that bad. Have fun, and get a snake for me."

As your friends leave, Caleb turns to you. "I'm glad you didn't go. Moses has been gone on the mountain for forty days and nights. It's the second time he has been gone that long." You both gaze up at the fiery mountaintop.

"Do you think he's still alive?" you ask.

"He's alive," Caleb says with a smile.

Just then, you see someone coming out of the cloud. It is Moses. He is carrying stone tablets. When you see his face, you and Caleb pull back in fear. Moses looks as though his whole face is lit up like lightning.

You both run back to the camp. Aaron and the others are afraid, too. Finally, Moses calls to all of you. First the leaders go toward him. They look like they could turn and run at any second. When they reach Moses, he talks to them. Finally, everyone finds the courage to go up to Moses. He shows you the law that God told him to write on the tablets. Then he tells you all the commands that God gave him for Israel. One of them is not to eat snakes.

As you listen to Moses, everything makes sense. It is good to tell the truth and to obey your parents. You think, "Why would I want to worship any god but the God of Israel? Who else has such power and such wisdom?"

When Moses is finished, he puts a veil over his face. From that time on, after every visit Moses has with God, his face glows, and he covers it with a veil.

What a wonderful God Israel has! His light shines so brightly that Moses' face shows it, too. You decide that you will follow your God all of your days. You have a good and exciting life.

THE END

While everyone is waiting for the warrior's return, you begin to back up and then start running away from the chariots, horses, and fierce looking soldiers. You run as fast as you can, not looking over your shoulder for fear that you are being followed.

You run and run, but the cloud does not seem to end. It is completely protecting the Israelites. God has kept his promise just like Moses said he would. He is protecting his people.

You hear chariot wheels moving behind you and an Egyptian soldier yells, "Stop, slave."

Having him so close scares you. You keep running. The last thing you remember is the pain of an arrow piercing your back. You fall forward, dead.

THE END

"No. I don't believe that melted earrings and necklaces can make a god," you say. "Pharaoh's idols didn't protect his army at the Red Sea. Grow up, Esau."

"I don't care what you say. Moses and his God are dead. Now we have a real god."

"Talk about dead! That golden calf isn't alive. It has no power at all."

"You're no fun anymore," Esau says. He walks away from you.

"You did the right thing," your mother says, coming out from the tent. "There's only one God, and that calf isn't it."

Mary and Mariah have been listening, and Mary pleads, "Mother, you don't understand. All our friends are over there. Can't we go, too?"

"No, you stay here with us."

Mariah stamps her foot, "But all our friends will think we're weird."

"Let them think what they want. This family will not have any part of idol worship. Is that clear? Stay on this side of the camp."

You try to hide your smile.

"Oh, all right," they mutter together.

A few days later as you are munching on a baked manna snack, your father runs into the tent. "Moses is back, and he is furious."

"I didn't do anything," Mariah says.

"She didn't, and I was with her the whole time," Mary adds. You laugh, but when you see the seriousness of your father's eyes, you stop.

"I want everyone to stay here for a while," your father says. "Don't leave this tent unless I come and get you."

You stay inside, but you can smell something burning. Later you hear yelling and the clanking of metal. When the noise is over, you learn that over 3,000 people were killed for turning their backs on God.

"Where's Esau?" you ask. Your father shakes his head. You continue, "Does that mean you don't know where he is?"

"It means," your father says slowly, "that Esau and his father are dead."

"No!" you cry.

You are angry at Moses and God because your friend died. Your father tries to comfort you, but you pull away. You go off by yourself to think.

CHOICE ONE: If you stay angry at Moses and God, go to page 53.

CHOICE TWO: If you trust God even though you are still confused by Esau's death, go to page 29.

You drop to the ground and ignore the stones digging into your ribs. You close your eyes and roll toward the man's legs to trip him. He loses his balance and falls on his sword right beside you. You feel his weight pressing against you. When you open your eyes, his blade is only two inches from your face. You are afraid to move.

The enemy soldier is dead. You gasp for air, but do not feel like you are getting enough. There is blood everywhere. You pass out.

You wake up when the battle is over. Esau finds you. He sneaked out of camp to make sure you were okay. He helps you home, and you tell him about everything that happened. Israel won the battle, and you are so grateful to be alive!

THE END

You are exhausted, but choose to meet your doom with your eyes open. On your way to your family's tent, you stumble near the shore. The water looks deep. You dip your hand in, and a shiver runs up your arm and down your back. You give up on the idea of swimming across. A light breeze is blowing. In the distance, you see that Moses has raised his staff and stretched his hand out over the water. The breeze changes to a strong east wind.

Something really strange is happening over near Moses. Waves have risen on the sea, but they are going in opposite directions, some to the left and the rest to the right! You give in to curiosity and move closer to Moses.

There seems to be a shallow trench going down the middle of the sea, all the way across to the other shore. You pull your cloak tightly around your body against the wind and try to protect your ears. The wind and waves are so loud that you would not be able to hear someone shouting right beside you.

The channel is getting deeper. A misty spray fills the air. Every now and then splashing water threatens to drench you. You move back, but not far enough. A wave slaps the side of the shore and drenches your legs. Again you back up. Water squishes in your sandals. As the trench deepens, the water on either side of it piles up like walls holding the rest of the sea back.

"So that's it!" you say to yourself. "God is making a path for us through the water." Then it dawns

on you. God is in charge of the wind and the clouds. He is even in charge of the Red Sea.

You run back to your family. "Mary! Mariah! Come see!" The girls must not have been sleeping soundly, for they both jump up at once.

"What is it? Are the Egyptians here?" Mary asks. "Oh, what will we do?"

"Don't be silly. Do you hear anyone screaming?" you ask.

Mariah calms down first. "Tell us what's happening."

"You won't believe until you see it. Follow me."

Just then your parents get up. "Hold it one minute, you three," your father says. "Help us break camp. Then you can go see whatever it is."

As you help pack your family's belongings, you keep glancing toward the sea. A crowd has started to gather near it. Finally, you and your sisters are free to go. You race over to the water's edge, dodging around people, animals, and belongings. When you arrive, you see that the trench now goes all the way down to the seabed. Instead of the muddy bottom that should be there, you see only a dry path through the sea.

"Yes!" you yell into the air as others also shout for joy. Mary and Mariah have caught up. Your father is not far behind. They join in the celebration, hugging and cheering. No one celebrates long, though. People at the front of the group grab their belongings and run toward the passage in the sea.

"Let's get your mother, the baby, and our things," your father shouts.

"But I'm scared!" Mary says. You hate it when she whines.

"What if the water caves in on us?" Mariah says. Looking at the towering water walls, you think she has a point.

"Mary and Mariah, there's no time for your dramatics," your dad says. "We're going to walk straight through that sea, because God has opened the way for us."

As you help your mother pack the final few blankets, she keeps repeating, "It's unbelievable!"

Esau's father yells back, "What's so unbelievable? These windstorms happen all the time. It's just a fluke. We need to hurry before the wind changes, though."

Mariah rolls her eyes at you. "He doesn't make sense. The wind couldn't do that by itself." You agree.

You help steady the cart as your father pushes it down to the seabed. The ground is solid and dry.

"Don't look up!" you hear Mariah say. Mary is trembling, staring at the monumental walls of water. Mariah is pulling her along. At first, you feel closed in. You just want to run back to the shore and forget this whole thing.

Your mind keeps asking, "What is holding the water up?" After you have gone about a third of the way through the sea, you look back. You wonder,

"What if the water starts falling in on me? Can I make it to the shore in time?" You wonder about this God who has called your people out of Egypt. Will he really protect you? You look at the wall of water on your right. Do you dare touch it? You can see fish swimming. Timidly, you reach out and touch the water. It feels cool and wet.

"The wind didn't do this," you say aloud. "God did it." You smile. Joy fills your heart. You help your father push the cart the rest of the way.

By the time you get across, you are hungry and extremely tired. Everyone is praising God. Women are singing and dancing with tambourines, but your eyes will not stay open another minute. You find a place to curl up and take a nap.

When you wake up, Esau is watching you. "How can you just sleep? Aren't you even hungry?"

"I suppose," you say.

"You think that just because we made it across the sea in a crazy windstorm that everything is fine?" he asks.

"What's wrong?" You rub your eyes and try to wake up completely.

"Where's the food?" Esau asks. "Where will we find food? We'll run out soon. I don't see any leeks or melons growing here. We'll starve in this desert." He stomps away from you.

CHOICE ONE: If you listen to Esau, go to page 38.

CHOICE TWO: If you ignore what he says, go to page 91.

"Thank you," you say. "I would appreciate traveling with you."

Before long, you learn different things that you can do to make Haran's life easier. You are happy to serve him because he is generous and very rich.

"I will be sad when you leave," Haran says.

"I don't have to go," you say. You like traveling with this nice man.

"Would you like to be one of my servants?" Haran asks.

"I would," you say. You know that Haran is getting older and probably does not need another servant. He is just being nice.

He smiles at you. "You will be my personal servant. I am making one last trip before I settle down and retire."

"I will go with you wherever you go," you say.

"When we have finished trading out goods on this trip," Haran says, "I plan to come back this way and settle in a city called Jericho. It has good strong walls and will be a safe place."

You smile. Life is so full of adventures. You miss your family, but you feel sure they are safe somewhere. Soon you settle in Jericho with Haran. You have a good life there for the next forty years.

THE END

It seems impossible that God can protect you from the Egyptians forever, even though he did bring plagues against Pharaoh and Egypt. Watching them try to chase frogs from their homes was pretty funny. You smile.

God has done so much for you already. What else can he do? Maybe Pharaoh's army will be crushed by a stampeding herd of wild camels. Or a sandstorm could bury them.

"How he does what he does is none of my business," you think. "The God who got me out of Egypt can keep me safe if he wants to." Your brain hurts from thinking. You decide to get some rest. You sleep peacefully until the sound of a ram's horn wakens you a few hours before dawn.

"Moses has given the order to break camp," your father says.

"Where are we going?" you ask.

"I don't know," your father says, "but look at what's happening to the Red Sea."

You cannot believe your eyes. The water of the sea has dammed up into walls on both sides. There is a path through the middle of the sea! People are beginning to walk across it to the other bank.

"Mother!" you call. "Come and look." She joins you at the tent's entrance. Wind blows through the opening into the tent.

"Oh, no! Help me!" cries Mariah.

You run to her. "What's wrong?"

"The wind is ruining my hair," she says.

You almost tell her that the wind could not make it look any worse than sleeping on it has.

Mary rubs her eyes as she stares out at the Red Sea. "I'm not going through there. What if the water falls and drowns us?"

Quickly, you help your father and sisters break everything down and pack up. You are so excited that God has given you an escape route. Your whole family walks through the sea together. Even as you travel with high water on either side of you, it feels more like a dream than reality. No matter how long you live, you will never forget the fishy smell of being in the middle of the Red Sea.

Once all of Israel is across, God looses the water on the chariots of the pursuing Egyptians. Soon the dead bodies of your former masters line the shore. You praise God with the rest of Israel.

After several weeks of travel in the desert, Israel again comes face-to-face with an enemy. A people called the Amalekites come out to attack. You hope that God will save your people again, just as he did at the Red Sea.

Moses sends Joshua and others to meet the Amalekites in a valley. The battle seems to go on for so long. You just have to know what is happening. As an excuse to see the action, you get water to bring to Moses. You see him standing on a high hill watching the battle. You cannot get close enough to give him the water, so you drink it and hide behind a boulder.

Some of the fighting moves right below you. There are several loose rocks by your feet. Maybe you can use them as weapons.

CHOICE ONE: If you just watch the battle, go to page 32.

CHOICE TWO: If you join the battle, go to page 54.

"No, I'm going to stay," you tell yourself. "I like the people with Haran better, but only here can I learn to serve the one true God."

"Who are you talking to?" Mary asks.

"Just myself," you say.

"You're weird," says Mariah. They both walk off, and all you can do is shake your head after them.

You do not let them stop you from talking, because you need to sort this out. "The God of Moses has saved my life and the lives of my family. It's enough for me just to know that he is God."

With that decided, you gather your manna for the day and then wander off toward Mount Sinai. You know it is forbidden to touch the mountain, but you want to get a little closer. You are curious about this God of Moses. As you near the base of the mountain, you notice someone looking up at it. It is no one you know.

You walk toward him. "See anything?"

"No," says the man. He turns to you. "You're Jacob's child aren't you, the one who was stuck on the wrong side of the sea?"

You laugh. "That's me."

"I'm Caleb," he says.

"It's pretty scary-looking up there, isn't it?"

Caleb turns around and sits on a rock. "There's a good reason for that. Our God is mightier than anything we can imagine."

"I know. I tried to run away from him at the Red Sea."

"I don't believe that you can hide from God," Caleb says. He spends a lot of time telling you about what God told Moses. You like Caleb. He is closer to your father's age, but he talks to you like you are an adult. And not once does he complain.

"There you are," Esau says. He, Ruth, Jaben, and some others come up behind you.

"We're tired of manna. Want to go snake hunting with us?"

CHOICE ONE: If you go snake hunting, go to page 22.

CHOICE TWO: If you stay with Caleb, go to page 64.

Even though your parents told you not to, you hang around with your usual crowd.

"It's so hot," Ruth says.

"I'm tired of Moses telling us what to do," says Jaben.

"I can't wait to get out of this desert and eat something besides manna," you say.

Most of the time, you are either listening to people complaining or you are grumbling yourself. Many of the people think Moses is dead. He has been on the burning mountain too long.

"Aaron, we want you to make us a new god," some say.

You wonder if that would be right. "Can people really make whatever god they want?" you wonder. Those who are asking for a god are fun to be around, and they seem to know so much more than you.

"We want gods like the Egyptians have," they cry. "Make us gods to lead us!" You join in their demand for gods you can see instead of one you cannot.

Aaron finally agrees. He collects gold jewelry from the people. Then he takes a tool and forms a golden idol in the shape of a calf.

The people are excited. "Look at our god who brought us up out of Egypt!" they shout.

You like being able to see your god. This god is pretty. It is made of shiny, valuable gold. Aaron builds an altar to the new god. He calls for a holiday the next day. Your parents are really upset about it.

"Don't go near that calf," your father says.

"It's evil," adds your mother. "This is not why God delivered us from Egypt."

"Don't worry about me," you say. "I'm just watching because I'm bored. I'm not touching it. Looking can't hurt."

"Don't go near it," your mother says.

The next morning many, many people get up early to celebrate. You watch from a distance. They offer sacrifices to the golden calf. Then they eat, drink, and do lots of things that you know are not right. You begin to wonder if you should even be watching.

Esau sees you and waves. "What are you doing way over there?"

"Just watching," you say.

"Why are you watching when you could be having fun?" Esau asks.

CHOICE ONE: If you hang back and continue watching, go to page 45.

CHOICE TWO: If you join the party in front of the golden calf, go to page 63.

CHOICE THREE: If you walk away, go to page 93.

You do not want to be caught by the Egyptians, but water standing straight up in the air makes you nervous. You run back in the direction you came, down the shoreline. At least you know what to expect along this beach. You run until you realize that the Egyptians are not chasing you.

Only then do you stop and turn around. All the Egyptian chariots have moved into the path through the Red Sea. You pray to the God of Moses to protect your family.

Just then, you hear a roar. In a moment, the path that was dry is completely filled with water. You blink, trying to take in what you just saw. You stand there, unmoving for some time, watching the wild waves where the Egyptian army once was.

"I can't believe what I just saw," you say to yourself. You cannot take your eyes from the spot. Israel's God is so powerful that he wiped out all the Egyptian charioteers in a single stroke.

The idea of a God being that powerful scares you. The Egyptians' gods did not have that much power. What if Moses' God wants to kill you for not trusting him? You plan to run away as far as you can. You do not want God to notice you, but where can you hide? You cannot go west or you will end up back in Egypt. You cannot go east because of the Red Sea. Perhaps you will find a trade route if you go north. Maybe you should go south and try to find someone with a boat to take you across.

CHOICE ONE: If you go south, go to page 88.

CHOICE TWO: If you go north, go to page 61.

You look at the faces of the soldiers in each chariot. They are fierce and hard—except for one. You rush up to him.

"Mercy," you cry. "Spare my life."

"Why should I spare your life?" he asks. "Are you my slave?"

"I am now." You are so scared that you do not even look up into his face.

"You agree to be my slave for the rest of your life?" he asks.

"I do," you say.

There is a long pause before he says, "Very well. It looks as if we'll make camp here until the dust storm moves on." You begin to help him set up camp as if your life depends on pleasing him, which it probably does.

That evening after you have fed your master his meal, your stomach is still growling for food. You notice that the cloud is dark on the Egyptian side. You wonder if it is light on the other side for the Israelites, as usual. The pillar of cloud changes to a pillar of fire every night for Israel. That way, the people always know God is with them.

You sigh. That night you go to sleep only after your master has. You sleep at his feet. The next morning, it is barely light when you hear shouts from others in the camp.

"The storm is lifting!"

You quickly help your master dress and pack his things. Within minutes he is in his chariot. You look toward where the cloud lifted, but the Israelites are not there.

"Where did they go?" you wonder.

"They'll not get away from us so easily," your master says. What could he mean? You look again. That is when you notice that the Red Sea has a path through it. God made a path through the Red Sea! All of your family and friends have crossed through the water on dry land. Amazing! Most of them are already across. The last of them are clear on the other side of the seabed, going up its banks. They look like ants, they are so far away.

Pharaoh's army gets into formation. The horses are ready for swift pursuit.

CHOICE ONE: If you move to the back of the army where the other servants and slaves are, go to page 55.

CHOICE TWO: If you jump on the back of your master's chariot, go to page 30.

You decide to keep going in the direction that you are already traveling. You are hoping that at some point, you will find a place to cross. Then you can travel back to meet up with your family. That is your goal anyway. When you finally reach a small village, you intend to stay there only a few days. One of the farmers in the area takes a liking to you.

"Why not stay here with us?" he says. You see that he needs help with his house, so you make bricks for him like you used to for the Egyptians.

When the people in the village realize that you know how to make the best bricks they have ever seen, they beg, "Do not leave us. You can make a good living for yourself here."

You think about their offer. "I'll stay for a while, but someday I must leave and find my family."

Life is relaxing in this village, and you like being paid for your work. You enjoy being treated like an adult, too. You like being known as the best brick maker in town. Later, you marry and have children of your own. As you grow older, you tell others of what you saw at the Red Sea. Everyone hears how powerful the God of Israel is.

THE END

You pick up food until your basket is full and set it by your bed. All day you snack on it. You cannot remember ever having so much food all to yourself. At night, you still have half a basket left. You do not want your mother to see it, and you do not want to have to share it with the twins, so you hide it under your blanket.

That night, you dream of eating sweet wafers under golden sunshine. At dawn, you are suddenly wide awake. A horrible smell makes you want to choke. Something is crawling on you. In fact, things are squirming all over you! You hop up and run out of the tent.

"What are you doing?" your father asks. You dance around trying to shake the bugs off. Your father follows you out into the morning light. "They're wormy maggots," he says.

"Oh no!" you exclaim. "Where did they come from?" You pick one out from between your toes.

Your father helps you brush them off. You go back into the tent. Your father holds the tent flap up to give you light. Maggots are all over your covers and mat.

"Where did they come from?" you ask.

"You didn't do what you were told." Your father points to your manna. Instead of wafers of bread, you have a basket crawling with maggots.

"I'm going to be sick." You run outside to throw up. After you clean yourself off, your father helps you shake your mat and covers. You clean the basket together, and then he makes you clean out the whole tent.

"God provided the manna for us to eat," your father says. "He told us not to save it, except on the Sabbath." His face gets stern. "Let's try trusting God and doing it his way from now on, okay?"

"Okay," you say.

From that day on, you only gather what you can eat in one day. Sometimes you even go a little hungry. The sight of manna almost makes you sick. You keep remembering that rotten smell and feeling the maggots crawling all over you. Manna never tastes quite as good to you again.

THE END

You ignore what Esau is saying. What you experienced today is too wonderful. You will not let him spoil it. Several days later, you are at a place called Marah, where God does another miracle for you. Moses tells all the Israelites to listen carefully to what the Lord tells them. He says to do what is right and to follow all God's commands. If you do, then God will protect you from the diseases that he brought on the Egyptians.

"For I am the Lord, who heals you," God says.

You believe it. Even though your feet are blistered and your face and hands are a little sunburned, you know that the Lord will keep his promise. He opened the Red Sea, didn't he? A God like that must really love you. You know that he can do anything!

THE END

You decide to throw yourself on Pharaoh's mercy. Hopefully, he is feeling kind today. The dust cloud in the distance draws closer to you. It is enormous.

"I know," you tell yourself, "maybe one of Pharaoh's soldiers will take me as his slave! Then I can beg for my family's lives, too." You hate the thought of being a slave again, but at least you will be alive. The idea makes more and more sense to you.

You hurry past the tents of the other Israelites and through the herds of goats in your way. The coast is clear. A twinge of fear runs down your back, and you hesitate. You look back in the direction of the camp. You love your family too much to let them die. If you can reach the Egyptians in time, you will beg for their lives and for your own.

You race toward the approaching Egyptian army. Suddenly, you realize that they are coming faster than you thought. What if they are moving too fast to see you?

CHOICE ONE: If you turn back, go to page 34.

CHOICE TWO: If you try to signal to them, go to page 47.

You shrug.

"Come down and join us," says Esau.

You want to be with your friends, but what they are doing is wrong. Inside, you wrestle with what to say next.

Esau continues, "Quit scowling and smile. Life's about having fun."

"No, Esau, it's not." You stand up.

"Don't tell me you're a Moses follower." Esau rolls his eyes.

"I'm a follower of God," you say. "If he wants me to follow Moses, then that's what I'll do. What you're doing is wrong. I'm going."

A strange expression rests on Esau's face and the faces of the two friends next to him. They look uncomfortable.

One of them, Simeon, says, "I think I'll come with you."

As you leave, Esau taunts, "Moses lovers. Moses lovers."

From then on, you and Simeon spend a lot of time together and become good friends. Forty years later, Simeon thanks you. "If you hadn't stood up for what was right when you did, I would have died with Esau instead of entering the Promised Land."

Joyfully, you cross the Jordan River together.

THE END

"Help! Help! We're going to die!" you scream. You and the twins run around in circles waving your hands in the air and kicking the sand. Suddenly, you run into one another, cracking heads. Pain shoots through your forehead. When you touch it, you feel a large gash. Your hand is covered with blood. You faint at the sight of it.

For a long time, you feel hot and far away. Every now and then you hear yourself cry out, "We're going to die!" When you finally wake, three days have passed. Everyone is safe. Was it all a dream? Did Pharaoh's army really come after you?

Mary and Mariah tell you an incredible story about walking on the bottom of the sea. They tend to exaggerate, so you don't believe them. Then your parents and friends tell the same story. Is this a joke? Are they trying to drive you crazy? Or did you sleep through the most awesome experience of your life?

You don't believe anyone until more miracles happen. Like when water comes from a rock and food falls from the sky. Then you're sorry you missed seeing the waters of the Red Sea part.

From now on, you're going to steer clear of Mary's and Mariah's heads.

THE END

Faith
Building
Guide

Ages
9 and up

Faith

Deadly Expedition!
Spiritual Building Block: **Faith**

You can do the following things to deepen your trust in our Father:

Think About It:

The Israelites were God's people. As often as they turned their back on him, he saved them. God was sad and angry that his people wandered from him, but he continued to give them opportunities to turn back to him. Think about the times God forgave you and welcomed you back even after you had made poor choices. Praise him for his grace and love.

Talk About It:

Telling others that you have committed your life to God not only cements your faith, it encourages others to grow in theirs. Ask your pastor or youth leader if you may give a testimony in church or Sunday school. The leader might want to hear what you plan to say and to help you come up with the right words.

Try It:

Sometimes God reveals his will in a very personal way. Sometimes he allows us to live within his general plan. Read the Bible and pray every day, alone and with others, to better understand God's plan for your life. Sometimes obeying God is difficult, but obedience always results in greater faith and a better life.

COLLECT THEM ALL!

ESCAPE!

Imagine that your decisions have the power to determine the fate of many Christians.

You have become a believer of Jesus Christ—even though you know you might die because of it. You see one of your favorite Christians, Stephen, being dragged off by temple officials to be killed for his faith. You must make a choice. You run off to warn your family that danger is coming. As you are leaving, you overhear people making plans to raid the home of your good friends. You must make a choice.

ATTACK!

Imagine that your decisions have the power to determine the fate of your country.

One day, while you are guarding your family's sheep, a bully attacks you from behind and steals your prized possession. You must make a choice. You abandon the sheep and chase the bully and almost catch him when you both see a huge foreign army in the distance. You must make a choice. Do you forget the differences you have with the bully, or work together to see what the foreigners are up to? You must make a choice.

TRAPPED!

Imagine that your decisions have the power to determine whether your family will be saved from its enemies.

Your Aunt Rahab is one of your favorite people, but your father doesn't want you to spend time with her. You must make a choice. When you visit her house you discover that the enemy of your people have been using her house as a hide-out! You must make a choice. Do you listen to Rahab's reasons for helping the spies? Do you believe her when she says that you must stay with her to be safe? Not everyone in your family believes her. You must make a choice.